GOBLIN at the beach

Victor Kelleher and
Stephen Michael King

RANDOM HOUSE AUSTRALIA

This one is for Lucius. V.K.

For Little Miss T, Ocean Boy and Red Gi[illegible]t. S.M.K.

A Random House book
Published by Random House Australia Pty Ltd
Level 3, 100 Pacific Highway, North Sydney NSW 2060
www.randomhouse.com.au

First published by Random House Australia in 2007
This edition published in 2010

Addresses for companies within the Random House Group can be found at www.randomhouse.com.au/offices.

National Library of Australia
Cataloguing-in-Publication Entry

Author: Kelleher, Victor, 1939–
Title: Goblin at the beach / Victor Kelleher;
illustrator Stephen Michael King
ISBN: 978 1 86471 955 0 (pbk.)
Series: Kelleher, Victor, 1939– Gibblewort the Goblin
Target Audience: For children
Subjects: Goblins – Juvenile fiction
Other Authors/Contributors: King, Stephen Michael
Dewey Number: A823.3

Cover illustration by Stephen Michael King
Cover design by Leanne Beattie
Internal design and typesetting by Stephen Michael King
Printed and bound by Griffin Press, South Australia

Random House Australia uses papers that are natural, renewable and recyclable products and made from wood grown in sustainable forests. The logging and manufacturing processes are expected to conform to the environmental regulations of the country of origin.

10 9 8 7 6 5 4 3 2 1

CHAPTER ONE

Gibblewort, the wicked Irish goblin, was lost somewhere in the Australian bush. He was searching for a post office, so he could mail himself back to Ireland. But he couldn't find one anywhere, and that made him grumpier than usual.

'Blither and blather!' he cried, and snapped at a passing fly. 'What a terrible country this is.'

He reached a dirt road just as a cattle truck came driving up.

'Goblins be praised!' said Gibblewort. 'I'm saved!'

'You're a funny lookin' bloke,' said the truckie. 'Are you a bunyip or somethin'?'

Gibblewort's voice rose to an angry squeak. 'Have you no eyes in your stupid head? Can you not see I'm a fine an' handsome goblin?'

'I don't know about the handsome part,' said the truckie, who didn't like the look of Gibblewort's hairy ears and brown fangs. 'In fact, you're too ugly to get in my cab.'

At the thought of being left behind, Gibblewort let out a sob. A green tear plopped into the dust.

'Take me with you, mister,' he begged. 'All I'm wantin' is a ride home to dear old Ireland.'

The driver scratched his head. 'Ireland's a bit far for me. Tell you what, climb in the back an' I'll drop you off at the coast. That'll get you started.'

Gibblewort had never heard of the coast. But by the sound of things, it was on the way home.

'You're a darlin' feller!' he crowed, and climbed aboard.

He didn't feel so pleased a moment later, when he found the truck full of frisky young bullocks.

He spent the rest of the journey being chased round and round the inside of the truck.

CHAPTER TWO

Gibblewort was a nervous wreck by the time they reached the coast. He toppled onto the side of the road the minute the truck stopped.

He nearly climbed back in again when he saw what lay before him.

'This isn't the way to Ireland!' he yelled. 'Why this is nothin' but a... a giant SANDPIT! With lots of silly people rushing round in their undies!'

'I'll have you know this here's a beautiful Aussie beach,' said the truckie, and drove away.

'What in blazes is a *beach*?' muttered Gibblewort.

He was about to stomp off after the truck when something caught his evil eye. An old lady feeding seagulls with scraps from a paper bag.

Gibblewort's tummy gave an empty rumble.

'I'm thinkin' it's time for a spot of dinner,' he said, and snatched the bag of scraps for himself.

CHAPTER THREE

It turned out that the gulls were hungrier than he was.

'Ow!' he yelled, as they pecked his bald head.

'Ooh!' he groaned, as they tweaked the warts on his nose.

'Here, keep your dinner!' he cried, flinging the bag away.

The truth was, he didn't care about the scraps any more. He had already spotted something far tastier. Not ice creams or fairyfloss - goblins don't like any of that stuff. No, he was casting greedy glances at the sunscreen lotion people were smearing on their bodies.

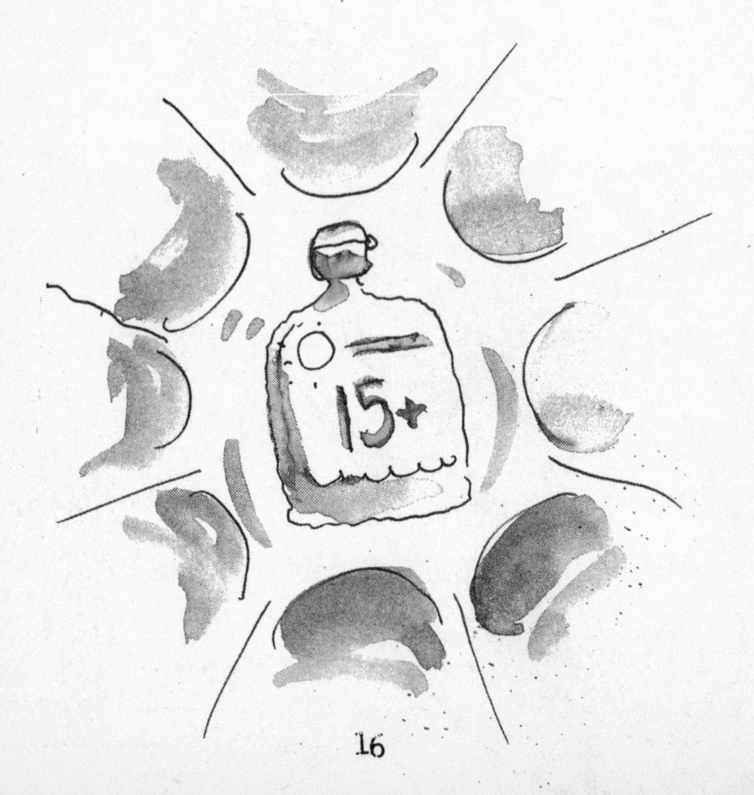

Taking off his shoes, so they wouldn't fill with sand, he ran onto the beach and snatched a bottle of lotion from a little girl.

This is the life! he thought, glugging it down. *Sure, it's the taste of heaven.*

He had nearly emptied the bottle when he noticed a funny smell. Then a sizzling sound. Like pork chops frying on a stove.

It was his own feet! They were burning up on the hot sand!

As everyone knows, goblins hate the feel of water. Yet that didn't stop Gibblewort.

'Psshhh!' went his feet, as he splashed into the shallows.

'Aaaahhh!' sighed Gibblewort, as steam rose up around him.

Pretty soon he was invisible, lost in a cloud of steam. So he didn't see the huge wave sweeping in.

With a whoosh, Gibblewort was upended. Then dragged out into deeper water where a family of crabs nipped him all over.

Up on the beach, the lifeguard saw a big green bubble burst from the sea.

'Yeeeeoowww-glub!' he heard someone scream.

The gulls are noisy today, he thought.

CHAPTER FOUR

When Gibblewort staggered from the waves, he was draped in slimy weed, and he had a fish flapping inside his shirt.

By now, he was in the worst mood ever. He stamped on buckets and spades. He kicked over sandcastles. He popped beach balls with his brown fangs. He pulled horrible faces to scare little kids. He took a pair of green armbands off a toddler and put them on his own arms, thinking they were goblin bracelets.

At last he was having fun. He searched around for other wicked things to do, and noticed that a crowd had gathered. A very angry crowd!

'Chuck that crazy monster off the beach!' someone yelled.

'Yeah, get rid of the little pest!'

Gibblewort went haring off, with the crowd close behind. Past the swimmers he ran; past the surfies and lifeguards; past the sunbathers and striped umbrellas; past the safety flag. But his feet kept sinking in the sand. The crowd was gaining steadily!

At the very last moment, he was saved by a fisherman. As the fisherman cast his line out to sea, the hook caught in a buttonhole on Gibblewort's shirt. The next minute he went sailing through the air.

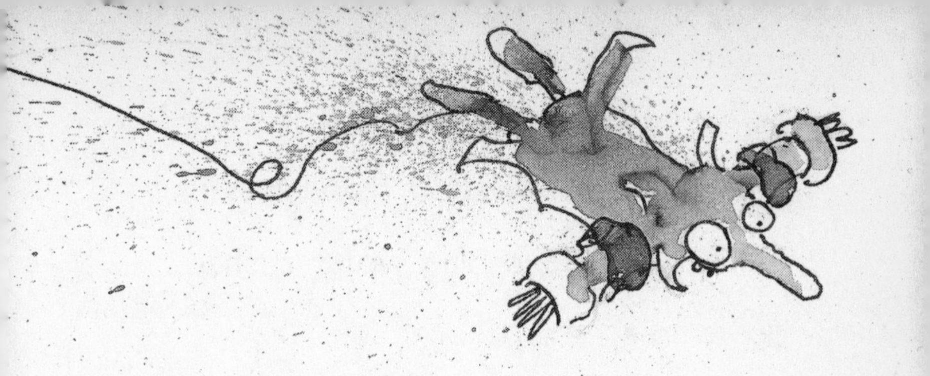

Out over the waves he flew. A cloud tickled his nose and made him sneeze. A butterfly landed on one hairy ear.

'Aah, it's not so bad up here,' sighed Gibblewort.

He was just starting to enjoy the view when the hook came free.

Down he plunged, faster and faster, until the wind whistled through gaps in his teeth. Deep blue water rushed up to meet him.

'Not two bathtimes in one day!' groaned Gibblewort.

CHAPTER FIVE

Gibblewort splashed nose first into the sea.

'Yuk-glub!' he complained, as the water closed above him.

By rights, his rock-hard head should have carried him to the bottom. But of course he was wearing his 'goblin bracelets' – the armbands he had stolen. So up he bobbed, like a cork.

'The goblin devils are watchin' over me this day,' he said. 'A bit of paddlin' an' I'll soon be out of this horrid bathtub.'

He was dreaming about being warm and dry, when some surfies sped past and splashed water into his eyes.

'Grrr-glub!' said Gibblewort, growing angry again.

Oh, how he longed to chase after them. How he wished he had one of those surfboards of his own.

He had no sooner made that wish than something bumped against him. It was long and floaty, just like a surfboard, so he climbed onto it.

Why, it even had a fin in the middle, to hold on to. And it sped away all on its own.

But why was it moving? There was no wave pushing it along. And weren't surfboards supposed to have their fins *underneath*? Also, who ever heard of a surfboard with *eyes*?

'Yikes!' cried Gibblewort.

'Click-click,' answered the dolphin, and caught the nearest wave.

Meanwhile, back at the beach, people were going wild.

'Wow! Check out that guy riding a dolphin!' they cried.

'Yeah, look at him go!'

The dolphin raced along, with Gibblewort clinging on for dear life.

'Someone get me off this terrible sea monster!' he pleaded.

The dolphin was happy to oblige. He'd had enough of smelly goblins. With a flick of his tail, he sent Gibblewort flying.

CHAPTER SIX

Gibblewort landed on a surfboard. Its rider was so surprised, that he fell off.

'Oh, dearie me!' squeaked Gibblewort, balancing on wobbly legs.

But worse was to come. With no one to steer it, the surfboard bumped into another surfboard and knocked that rider off too. To keep his balance, Gibblewort planted a foot on the second board. Now he was riding both surfboards at once!

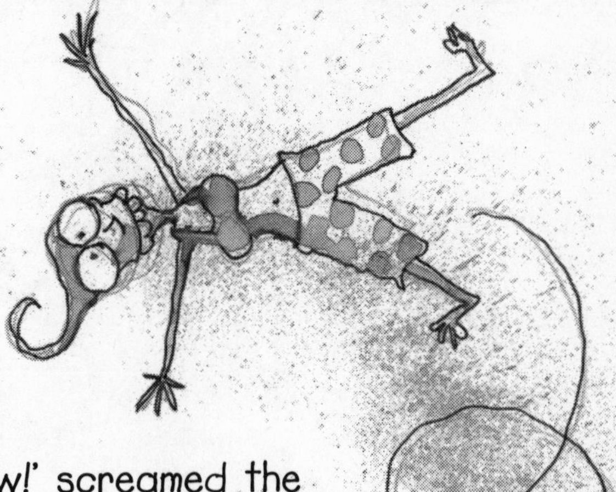

'Wow!' screamed the people on the beach. 'This guy gets better and better!'

'Yeah, he *must* be world champion!'

Right at that moment, he was world champion at doing the splits! As the two boards moved further and further apart, Gibblewort felt he was being torn in two. So were his trousers, that ripped down the middle.

'I can't stand much more of this!' he groaned, and toppled backwards... only to land on a boogie board!

Once again, the surprised rider fell off. Gibblewort was left to surf in alone. Clutching onto his ripped trousers (to stop them falling down!), he waded slowly through the shallows.

A big crowd was waiting further up the beach. The same crowd that had chased him only minutes earlier.

'I'm sorry, fellers...' he began, and stopped – because these people weren't angry at all.

They were cheering. Better still, they were cheering **HIM!** He was famous again – more famous than he'd been up in the mountains. And oh, how Gibblewort loved fame! It was his favourite thing. Better by far than other favourites, like snail and slug pie.

Admiring people gathered around, and he puffed out his chest with pride. Then wished he hadn't, when the leader of the surfies pinned a medal on him.

'Ow!' said Gibblewort.

'Sorry, bro,' said the leader, 'but you're the best.'

'Yeah, the greatest!' his mates agreed, and lifted Gibblewort shoulder high.

Gibblewort felt he had woken up in goblin heaven.

'Haven't I always known I was the greatest?' he sighed. 'It's *just* taken the world a while to discover me.' With a vain smile on his wicked face, he closed his eyes and lay back.

He didn't see the kite swoop down – one of those fast, buzzy kites that look like planes. Its pointy end hooked under his collar. Up into the air he shot. Out over the waves he sailed.

'Atchoo!' he sneezed, when he brushed a cloud.

The same butterfly as before landed

on one hairy ear.

Gibblewort seemed to float for a while. Then, with a buzzy jerk, the kite pulled free.

Oh no! thought Gibblewort.

CHAPTER SEVEN

Gibblewort landed in a school of jellyfish. Instead of making a splash, he bounced around on their rubbery bodies.

'Sure, these fellers are more springy than my bed back home,' he said. 'And a sight more comfy.'

He didn't find them quite so comfy when he was stung on the toe.

'Yow!' said Gibblewort.

Then **'Ooh!'** and **'Ouch!'** as he was stung on both knobbly knees.

Gibblewort bounced as high and as far away from the jellyfish as he could get.

Directly below, in open water, he could see a long grey shape. Could it be his old friend, the dolphin?

He landed neatly on its back, and took a firm grip of its dorsal fin.

'Ah, you're a darlin',' he crowed. 'You've saved me from the watery deep. Now I'll thank you to carry me safely to shore.'

The dolphin didn't reply. It gave an angry wriggle. Then it slapped the water with its tail.

Gibblewort glanced behind him. Had the dolphin's tail been quite that big? Or its dorsal fin so tall? Or its mouth so full of large, pointy teeth?

Gibblewort was standing on a shark! A very angry shark that raced through the water, trying to shake Gibblewort loose.

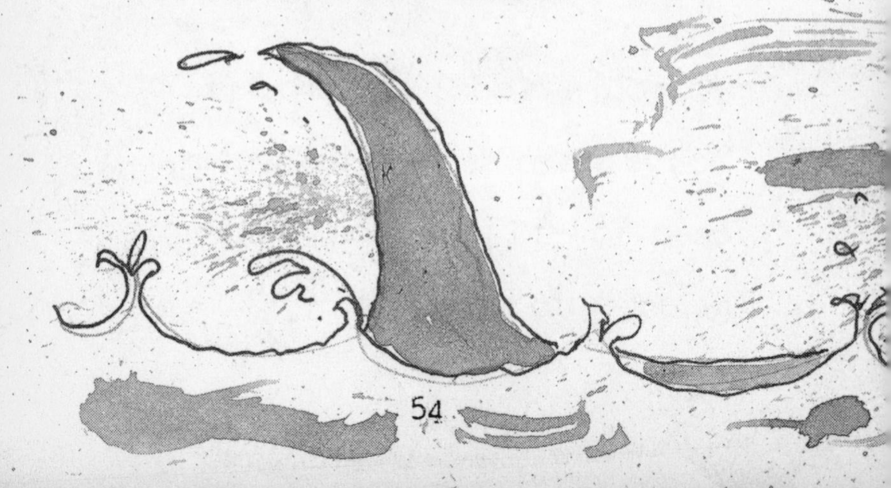

Back on the beach, people were cheering again.

'Wow! Look at him now! He's riding a shark!'

'Yeah, a white pointer!'

'What a hero. He's not afraid of anything.'

Gibblewort was more than afraid. He was terrified! He would have jumped clear if he could, but one of his armbands had slipped over the shark's dorsal fin. He was stuck there on its back!

The shark tried diving deep. It turned over and over. It swam in circles. It zoomed out of the water. It plunged into waves. But nothing could dislodge Gibblewort.

Pretty soon, the shark grew desperate. It was ready to do anything to get rid of this smelly creature. Even swim through the surf and up onto the shore.

There, Gibblewort managed to unhook his armband.

The shark, free at last, flipped back into the water and swam far out to sea, never to be spotted again.

CHAPTER EIGHT

The crowd that greeted Gibblewort was more excited than ever.

'You really are the greatest!' they shouted.

'Yeah, no one's ridden a shark before.'

The lifeguards were specially impressed. Their leader pinned another medal on Gibblewort's chest.

'Ouch!' said Gibblewort.

'This is for scaring off that shark,' the leader said.

Gibblewort was super famous now. But before he could enjoy his fame, his nasty little eyes noticed something gleaming in the sand. A whole lot of shiny blue beads.

Now everyone knows that goblins are the greediest creatures in the world. They LOVE to collect precious jewels. So at the sight of the beads, Gibblewort forgot about fame. With both greedy hands, he gathered them up, but they just popped when he touched them. They had strings attached, which tangled around his arms and legs.

Poor old Gibblewort didn't know about bluebottles and how they can sting. He soon learned.

'YEEEE!' he screamed, and began jumping up and down.

'Wow!' said the people in the crowd. 'He's a champion dancer too!'

'Yeah, what do you call that dance? An Irish jig?'

Gibblewort didn't care about jigs or anything else. He only wanted the stinging to stop. He reckoned that maybe cool water would help, and he rushed back into the surf. 'Wow!' yelled the crowd. 'Look at him swim! He's jet-propelled!'

Still kicking and squirming, he shot out through the waves. He didn't slow down until he reached calm water. There, at last, the soreness went away.

He looked with longing eyes at the distant beach. He wished with all his wicked heart that he was back there, being adored by his fans.

But before he could start the long swim, a ring of bubbles rose from the deep. They were followed by a humpback whale that surfaced beneath him!

'Wow!' shrieked the crowd. 'This guy can do anything. He's riding a whale now!'

He didn't ride it for long. The smell of goblin feet was too much even for a whale. With a slap of its tail, it tossed Gibblewort further out to sea.

CHAPTER NINE

Gibblewort splashed down amongst floating driftwood. Wearily, he dragged himself onto a big log with lots of sticking out branches.

Over on the horizon, he could see great ships. He wondered if they were headed for Ireland. Taking off his coat, he hooked it onto one of the branches, as a sail.

'I'll maybe ask them for a lift home to my soggy treehouse,' he said with a sigh.

But already the sun was setting. Also, there was something Gibblewort didn't know – he'd been badly sunburned on the beach. As darkness fell, he began to glow a bright red.

When the ships' captains saw his nose glowing in the dark, they took it for a danger signal.

'Here I am, fellers,' Gibblewort called hopefully, but it did no good.

The ships sailed away at top speed.

Tired out, Gibblewort settled down for a snooze.

'With a bit of goblin luck, I'll sail home meself,' he muttered drowsily.

The very next morning, it seemed as though he had. For in the night, the log had drifted towards land and then up a long river valley. So that when he awoke, he was surrounded by green rolling hills. There was even misty rain falling from a grey sky.

'Glory be to goblins!' cried Gibblewort. 'I'm back in my darlin' old Ireland.'

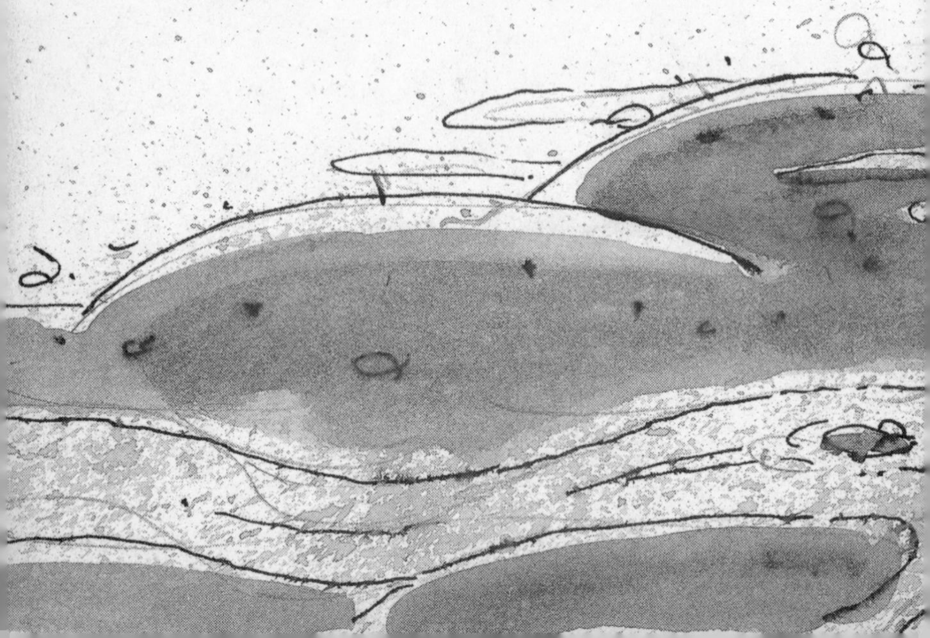

Splashing ashore, he set out through the rain, in search of his soggy treehouse.

What he didn't notice, high in a tree, was the watchful face of a koala.

Poor old Gibblewort! He'd landed in Australia again.

The Author

Victor Kelleher

Victor Kelleher was born in London and came to Australia in 1976 via Africa and New Zealand. After an academic career he now writes both children's and adults' novels full-time. His novels for Random House Australia include *To The Dark Tower, Del-Del, Beyond the Dusk* and the popular *Goblin* series with Stephen Michael King. Victor has been shortlisted for many awards including the Children's Book Council of Australia Book of the Year Award and the Australian Science Fiction Achievement Award. He remains one of Australia's most celebrated authors.

The Illustrator

Stephen Michael King

Stephen Michael King left school to pursue a career in nothing much. Trying to emulate Vincent Van Gogh, he twice dropped out of art school, eventually finding a job that suited him as a children's library assistant. After three years hanging out in the mind of a child, he moved into the serious world of the Walt Disney Sydney studios, before having his first book published – a 'how to draw cartoon animals' book. His first picture book, *The Man Who Loved Boxes*, won the Australian Family Therapists' Award and was selected for Pick of the List (US). He has been shortlisted many times for the Children's Book Council Book of the Year Awards and won both the 2002 YABBA and KOALA children's choice awards for *Pocket Dogs*.